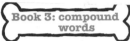

**Ph** **Reading Program** Book 3: compound words

# Get That Lunch Box

by Donna Taylor

Illustrated by José Maria Cardona

Based on the books by Norman Bridwell

SCHOLASTIC INC.

New York   Toronto   London   Auckland   Sydney
Mexico City   New Delhi   Hong Kong   Buenos Aires

"Emily Elizabeth," said Mrs. Howard, "please drop this letter in the mailbox on your way to school."

"Sure," said Emily Elizabeth. She put the letter in her backpack. Then she picked up her lunch box.

At the mailbox,
Emily Elizabeth put down
her lunch box.
She dropped the letter
into the mailbox.
Then she went to school.

Mac, Jetta's dog, saw
the lunch box.
Sniff! Sniff!
Mac smelled a
peanut-butter sandwich.

He tried to open
the lunch box.
He wanted to eat
that lunch.
But the lunch box
would not open.

Clifford saw Mac trying to
open the lunch box.
"No, Mac! Please leave
it alone.
That lunch box belongs to
Emily Elizabeth," he said.
"I must bring it to her
at school."

"Clifford, I want to eat this lunch," Mac said. "It smells good."

"If you eat it, Emily Elizabeth will be hungry later," Clifford said. "Give it to me, please."

Mac gave Clifford the lunch box.

Clifford ran to the schoolhouse.
When Emily Elizabeth got to school, Clifford was already there. He gave her the lunch box.

"Oh, my lunch box!" said Emily Elizabeth. "I must have left it at the mailbox. Thank you, Clifford."

# The Singing Birds' Show

by Suzanne Weyn

Illustrated by Angel Rodriguez

Based on the books by Norman Bridwell

SCHOLASTIC INC.
New York   Toronto   London   Auckland   Sydney
Mexico City   New Delhi   Hong Kong   Buenos Aires

Emily Elizabeth twirled in her yard.
She sang her favorite song. Little birds sang along.

Her friend Charley came by. "I like the way you sing," he said.

"Thanks," said Emily Elizabeth. "It must be fun to be a singing star."

"I just learned to play this guitar," said Charley. "We could sing and I could play along. We might even earn some money that way."

Emily Elizabeth and Charley went over their songs. Soon they learned to sing and play together.

First they put up a sign. Then they waited for people to come.
But no one came...
except Clifford.

"No one knows we're here," Emily Elizabeth said.

"Too bad we can't drive a car," said Charley. "Then we could go all over Birdwell Island to where the people are."

"I have an idea!" said Emily Elizabeth.

Emily Elizabeth and Charley got up onto Clifford's back.

"Please take us to the dock, Clifford," Emily Elizabeth said.

Clifford got going. He carried them to the ferry dock.
There were all sorts of people there.

Charley played and he and Emily Elizabeth sang. Clifford served as the stage.

When they were done, everyone clapped. Emily Elizabeth and Charley also earned money at the dock.

Then Clifford took them from there to the park and after that he took them into town.

"Thank you, Clifford," Emily Elizabeth said.

"You took us far so we could feel like real..."

# Clifford the Salesman

by Donna Taylor

Illustrated by Segundo Garcia

Based on the books by Norman Bridwell

SCHOLASTIC INC.
New York   Toronto   London   Auckland   Sydney
Mexico City   New Delhi   Hong Kong   Buenos Aires

"Emily Elizabeth," said
Mrs. Howard.
"Will you work in the front
of the shop for a while?
I have to work in the
back room."

"Sure," said
Emily Elizabeth. "I will
take good care of
the store."

Emily Elizabeth liked to help out at the store.

First, she put new cards in the rack.

Then she dusted the lamps. She put some of the Birdwell Island mats in the window. Then she added some seashells.

"Now I wish someone would come to shop," said Emily Elizabeth.

Soon Mr. Bleakman
came by.
He wanted to go inside
the store.
But Clifford was napping
right in front of the door!

"Move!" said
Mr. Bleakman.

Clifford just snored.

Mr. Bleakman yelled to Emily Elizabeth, "Your Big Red Dog is in the way!"

Emily Elizabeth came to the door just as Clifford moved his tail.

"Clifford must be dreaming," she said.

Clifford moved his
tail again.
Swat! This time his tail hit
the grocery cart.
Down, down the hill
it went.

"Oh, no!" yelled
Mr. Bleakman. "My eggs,
my eggs! They will
all break!"

Clifford woke up.
He saw the egg carton
fly in the air.
Away he went, chasing it!

He got the egg carton.
He got the eggs.
Not one broke.

"Thank you," said
Mr. Bleakman.

Then Mr. Bleakman went
into the shop.
He was in a good
mood now.
He bought six mats, five
seashells, and a lamp.

"What a good salesman you are!" said Emily Elizabeth.

# Spring Is in the Air

by Francie Alexander

Illustrated by Ken Edwards

Based on the books by Norman Bridwell

SCHOLASTIC INC.
New York   Toronto   London   Auckland   Sydney
Mexico City   New Delhi   Hong Kong   Buenos Aires

Clifford and
Emily Elizabeth go to
Clifford's doghouse.
They like to do things
together.

"It's story time, Clifford!"
says Emily Elizabeth.
Emily Elizabeth likes to
share books with Clifford.
They are quite a pair.

Emily Elizabeth sits on a chair. Clifford settles on the rug. She reads:

Spring Is in the Air

By
Bunny Hare

Emily Elizabeth reads:

Spring is in the air.
See the frogs leap.
They don't have
a care.

Clifford looks at the pictures.

Spring is in the air.
See green grass
all around.
The bear leaves
his cave.

Emily Elizabeth reads another page.

Spring is in the air.
Baby robins are
in a nest.
The foal is with its
mother, the mare.

Clifford wants to see
spring for himself.
Emily Elizabeth
does, too.

They go to the lake
together and find a nest.
But there are no eggs
inside. They wonder what
bird built this big nest.

Along comes a duck with fuzzy yellow ducklings. This is their nest.

The ducklings run behind their mother.
A soft yellow feather floats on a breeze.

Now Clifford and Emily Elizabeth know it's true...

Spring is in the air!

# Jumping in Puddles

### by Liz Mills

### Illustrated by Carolyn Bracken
### and Sandrina Kurtz

Based on the books by Norman Bridwell

SCHOLASTIC INC.
New York   Toronto   London   Auckland   Sydney
Mexico City   New Delhi   Hong Kong   Buenos Aires

It had rained the night before.

T-Bone saw puddles everywhere.

Today would be a good day to jump in puddles.

He decided to find his friends.

"Cleo, do you want to jump in puddles with me?" asked T-Bone.

"No," said Cleo. "I don't want to get wet and muddy. You go ahead, T-Bone."

"Okay," said T-Bone. "But I'm sorry you're not coming to play with me."

Then T-Bone went to
visit Mac.
"Mac, would you come
jump in puddles with
me?" asked T-Bone.

"No," said Mac. "I want to
take a nap. I'm sleepy."
And Mac went back
to sleep.

"Clifford, will you jump in puddles with me?" asked T-Bone.

"I'd like to," said Clifford. "But I won't fit in a puddle."

"You can still play. I've got an idea!" said T-Bone.

And so they walked to the park.

"Isn't this fun, Clifford?" asked T-Bone as he slid off Clifford's tail and jumped into a puddle.

"Yes, it's lots of fun," said Clifford. "I'm glad we're puddle jumping together."

Mac walked into the park.

"Hi, T-Bone," said Mac. "Hi, Clifford. Hi, Cleo."

"Didn't you want to take a nap, Mac?" asked T-Bone.

"I'm not tired anymore. And now I would like to jump into puddles!"

Puddle jumping is
best with friends!

# Good Sports

## by Francie Alexander
## Illustrated by Jim Durk

Based on the books by Norman Bridwell

SCHOLASTIC INC.
New York   Toronto   London   Auckland   Sydney
Mexico City   New Delhi   Hong Kong   Buenos Aires

It was a nice morning.

"I want to go to the seashore," said Cleo.

"Good idea!" said Clifford.

"Here we go!" said T-Bone.

On the way to the shore,
the dogs heard a horn.
Cleo jumped in surprise
and stepped on a thorn.

"Do you want to stop?" asked T-Bone.

"No, I want to go to the shore," said Cleo.

"You are a good sport," said Clifford.

On the way to the shore,
the dogs saw a fort.
They smelled popcorn
and they heard the ferry
blow its horn.

"What a fun day!"
said Clifford.

Gray clouds started
to form.

Clifford gave Cleo and
T-Bone a lift.
They raced home away
from the storm.

"Thanks, Clifford,"
said Cleo.

"You are a good sport,"
said T-Bone.

When they got to
Clifford's home,
Emily Elizabeth said,
"Come on, get out
of the storm!"

"Is our fun day over?"
T-Bone asked.

"No!" said Clifford. "We
will find more fun inside."

EMILY ELIZABETH'S S'MORES

Take a graham cracker.

Put a marshmallow on top.

Put one more graham cracker on top.

Eat one and you will want s'more.

She invited them in
for s'mores.

The dogs went inside and
had even more fun.

They were good sports.
Yum!

# A Little Book About Red

by Francie Alexander

Illustrated by Steve Haefele

Based on the books by Norman Bridwell

SCHOLASTIC INC.
New York  Toronto  London  Auckland  Sydney
Mexico City  New Delhi  Hong Kong  Buenos Aires

Time to get up!

Clifford barks at
the window for
Emily Elizabeth to get up.

She giggles and hops
out of bed.
It is cold so she puts on
fuzzy red slippers.

Emily Elizabeth likes red.

The kettle makes a loud whistle.

Emily Elizabeth runs to the table.
She has a little red hat on her head.
She has big red boots on her feet.

Emily Elizabeth likes red.

Emily Elizabeth and
Clifford go to school.
Clifford keeps her out
of the puddles.
She snuggles and pats
his head.
"Thank you for keeping
my red boots clean."
Emily Elizabeth likes red.

Today Emily Elizabeth's class visits the fire station.
It is so cold that the kids wiggle into their jackets.

"Welcome!" says Fire Chief Campbell.

Miss Carrington blows her whistle. "Stay in line," she tells the class.

"Look at the bright red fire truck,"
Miss Carrington says.

Fire Chief Campbell lets them climb on the truck.

What fun!

Emily Elizabeth likes red.

Back at school, the kids
settle down.
They read books and
do riddles.
They get red paper
and crayons.

Emily Elizabeth likes red.

Phonics Fun

Reading Program  Book 7: s, es

# I Spy a Big Red Dog

by Annie McDonnell

Illustrated by Barry Goldberg

Based on the books by Norman Bridwell

SCHOLASTIC INC.
New York  Toronto  London  Auckland  Sydney
Mexico City  New Delhi  Hong Kong  Buenos Aires

"Do you want to play a game?" asked Cleo.

Both Clifford and T-Bone said yes.

"I will start," said Cleo. "Do you see a ball?"

Can *you* find the ball?

"I spied a ball on my first try!" said Clifford.

"Good for you! What else can we spot?" said Cleo.

The friends walked around town.

"Do you see a butterfly?" asked T-Bone.

"I spy two beautiful butterflies!" said Cleo.

Can *you* find the two butterflies?

Clifford, Cleo, and
T-Bone ran to the beach.

"Do you see a bunny?"
Clifford asked.

"I spy three cloud
bunnies in the sky!"
said T-Bone.

"Bunnies at the beach!"
said Cleo. "How funny!"

Can *you* find the three
cloud bunnies?

"My turn now," said Cleo. "Do you see a seashell?"

"I spy two seashells near that guy," said Clifford.

"And I spy two seashells over there," said T-Bone. "That makes four seashells."

Can *you* find four seashells?

"Do you smell something good?" asked T-Bone.

"I smell apples," said Clifford.

Clifford, Cleo, and T-Bone followed the smell to the boardwalk.

"Do you see a dish?" asked Cleo.

"I spy five dishes of pie!" said T-Bone. "Yum!"

Can *you* find five pies?

The three dogs went to play in the park.

"Do you see a bird?" asked T-Bone.

"I spy six birds up high!" said Cleo.
"Look at the baby birds."

"The babies are so cute," said Clifford.

Can *you* find six birds?

"I spy a Big Red Dog going bye-bye!"

# Emily Elizabeth Can't Trade

### by Jenny Markas

### Illustrated by Josie Yee

Based on the books by Norman Bridwell

**SCHOLASTIC INC.**
New York   Toronto   London   Auckland   Sydney
Mexico City   New Delhi   Hong Kong   Buenos Aires

Emily Elizabeth was in a big rush.

"My friends are trading things today after school!" she said. "I can't find a thing to trade."

"You need to go, Emily Elizabeth," her mother said. "You will be late if you don't go now."

Emily Elizabeth got to school just in time.

At lunchtime, she looked around for something to trade.
*I wonder if I can trade this flower,* she thought. *It's really very nice.*

*No, I don't think so*,
she decided.
*This flower doesn't look
too good anymore.*

What would her friends
like to trade?
She looked all around but
couldn't find anything.

"I have the best cookies," said Charley that afternoon when school was done. "I'll trade one cookie for something."

"I have a toy snake to trade," said Jetta.

"It's a deal," Charley said. He gave her a cookie. Jetta gave him her toy snake.

"I can't trade!"
Emily Elizabeth told
Charley and Jetta.
"I didn't bring a thing
to trade."

"Do you want a cookie?"
Charley asked.
"I'll give it to you."

"No, thanks," said
Emily Elizabeth. "I want
to trade for one."

Clifford came along.
He had a present for
Emily Elizabeth.
It was a shiny rock.
He had found it on
the beach.

"Thanks, Clifford,"
said Emily Elizabeth.

"Now you have something to trade!" Jetta said. "I will trade this pack of cards for that rock. I'll add a marble to it."

Emily Elizabeth liked the cards. She liked the marble, too.

"Thanks, but I can't trade this rock," she said. "It's from my pal Clifford. That makes it too special to trade."

# Clifford and the Squirrel

by Janelle Cherrington

Illustrated by Robin Cuddy

Based on the books by Norman Bridwell

SCHOLASTIC INC.
New York   Toronto   London   Auckland   Sydney
Mexico City   New Delhi   Hong Kong   Buenos Aires

In spring, Emily Elizabeth said, "Charley, let's plant a garden. We can grow sunflowers."

"That's a great idea!" Charley said. "Let's plant carrots, watermelons, and cantaloupes, too."

First they took a gardening lesson from Mrs. Diller.

Then they loaded up Emily Elizabeth's wagon with shovels, wooden stakes, and packets of seeds.
Before long, the garden was planted!

"Soon we'll have lots of great plants," said Emily Elizabeth.

Emily Elizabeth and Charley went often to check on their garden. Each time, they brought a gallon of water for the plants. Soon, little seedlings came up, but only a few.

"We planted more seeds than this," said Emily Elizabeth. "I wonder why they aren't growing."

The children tried again.

They dropped more seeds in the ground. They weeded and watered. Still, the plants did not grow.

"I don't think this is right," Charley said.

Then one day, Emily Elizabeth saw the reason – a squirrel was eating all their seeds!

"I beg your pardon," Emily Elizabeth said. "It's not polite to eat seeds from my garden!"

But the squirrel just looked at her.
It kept right on eating.

Charley had an idea.
"We can make a
scarecrow," he said.

"Don't you mean a scare
squirrel?" Emily Elizabeth
said with a laugh.

But it didn't work.
That squirrel wasn't
scared at all.

Clifford knew Emily
Elizabeth was upset.
He wanted to help.
He knew what to do.

He talked to that squirrel.
"Listen," Clifford began.
"I will help you reach nuts
in all those trees if you
leave Emily Elizabeth's
garden alone."

The squirrel said, "It's
a deal!"

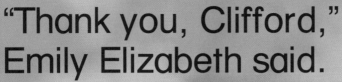

"Thank you, Clifford,"
Emily Elizabeth said.

# Mac the Knight

by Leslie McGuire

Illustrated by Thompson Bros.

Based on the books by Norman Bridwell

SCHOLASTIC INC.
New York   Toronto   London   Auckland   Sydney
Mexico City   New Delhi   Hong Kong   Buenos Aires

CLANK! BONK!
CLATTER! CLINK!

"What is all that noise?"
asked Cleo. Clifford
looked up just in time
to see an odd pile of
old tin cans go by.

"I know!" said T-Bone.
"That's Mac!"

"That's right!" said Mac.
"I am Mac the Knight.
Do you want to be in
my play?"

"Who wrote the play?" asked Cleo.

"I did," said Mac. "I am a knight who never gets things wrong. I save the pretty princess, too."

"Can I be the pretty princess?" asked Cleo.

"Yes," said Mac. "T-Bone can be the bad wizard, and Clifford can be the dragon who has her trapped in this tree!"

Mac started to wind a chain around Cleo, but his leg got stuck. Mac fell down on his knees.

CLATTER! CLANK! BONK! CLINK!

"This chain is too big," said Mac. "I have to use a rope." But Mac could not make a knot with all the cans on his paws.

"I will wrap it tight for you," said T-Bone.

"Now I will take this knife to cut the rope and save the pretty princess," said Mac. But Mac's knife was made of wood. The wood broke and knocked Mac on the wrist. CLONK! CLINK! BONK!

Cleo started to giggle.

"No giggling!" yelled Mac. "That will wreck my play!"

"I know," said Clifford. "The knight should wind Cleo's magic shawl around the mysterious wizard." But Mac's head got wrapped up in the shawl. CLINK! CLANK! CLONK! BONK!

Mac did not know
what to do.

"This play is turning out
all wrong," he said. "The
knight has not done one
thing right yet! All he
does is wreck things!"

"Don't be so sad," said
Clifford. "We can write a
new play!"

They helped Mac take off all the tin cans.

CLATTER! BONK! BONK! CLINK!

Then they sat down to write another play.

This play was about four smart dogs who make a magic race car out of tin cans. The car is so fast they win all the big racing prizes.

"Writing plays is fun!"
said Mac. "Let's write
another one."

# Cleo's
# Fudge Cakes

by Leslie McGuire

Illustrated by Gita Lloyd and Eric Binder

Based on the books by Norman Bridwell

SCHOLASTIC INC.
New York   Toronto   London   Auckland   Sydney
Mexico City   New Delhi   Hong Kong   Buenos Aires

"Today I will sell all my fudge cakes and get some money!" said Cleo.

Cleo put her fudge cakes on a log.
That was when T-Bone and Mac came over the bridge.

"Try my fudge cakes," said Cleo.

"I will trade you my badge for a fudge cake," said T-Bone.

"Where did you get so much fudge?"
asked Mac.

"Dogs should not eat fudge," said Cleo. "So I made my cakes with mud! Try one!"

"No, thank you," said T-Bone and Mac.

Cleo tried to sell her "fudge" cakes for the rest of the day.
No one seemed to want them.

"I will move to some other place to sell my fudge cakes," said Cleo. She pushed, but she could not make the log budge.

Then Clifford came by.

"Will you help me move this log? I will give you a fudge cake," Cleo said.

Clifford sniffed the cake. "No, thank you," he said. Clifford dragged the log for Cleo.

A cat and a bunny came over.

"Try my yummy fudge cakes," said Cleo.

The bunny sniffed the cakes.

"These are mud cakes," he said. "I only eat carrot cake!"

"I do not want mud!" said the cat. "I only eat fish cake!"

"I need some other place
to sell the cakes,"
said Cleo.

"Let's go to the lake!"
Clifford said.

"Who will want cakes at
the lake?" asked Cleo.

"You will see,"
said Clifford.

"Yum! Mud cakes!" said the ducks at the lake.

"We love mud cakes," said the frogs.

"Try our mud cakes," said Cleo.

"Yum!" said the ducks and frogs.

"See!" said Cleo. "Mud fudge cakes are great!"

"Right," said Clifford.
"They are great for
ducks and frogs!"